TRUCKS!
(and other things with wheels)

THIS IS A WELBECK CHILDREN'S BOOK

Published in 2020 by Welbeck Children's Books
An imprint of Welbeck Children's Limited, part of Welbeck Publishing Group
20 Mortimer Street, London W1T 3JW

Associate Publisher: Laura Knowles
Editor: Jenni Lazell
Design Manager: Emily Clarke
Designer: Dani Lurie
Production: Gary Hayes

A CIP catalogue record for this book is available from
the British Library.

ISBN: 978-1-78312-568-5

Printed in China

10 9 8 7 6 5 4 3 2 1

WELBECK

TRUCKS!
(and other things with wheels)

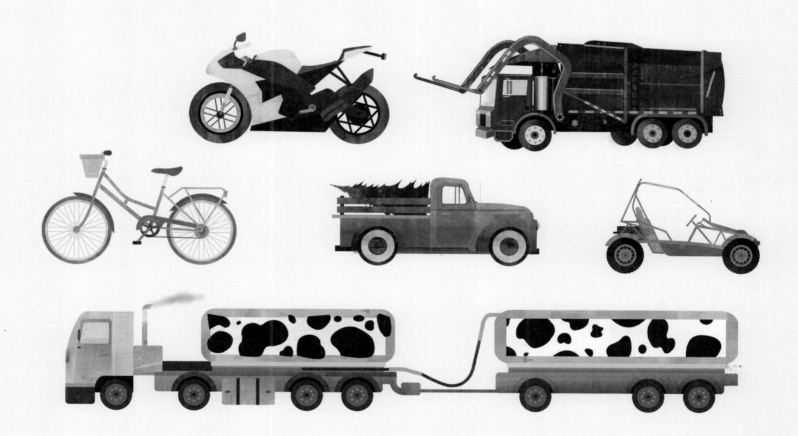

Written by
Bryony Davies

Illustrated by
Maria Brzozowska

This book belongs to:

....

Contents

Farm truck

Flatbed truck carrying pipes

Skip loader

Monster trucks can do tricks and jumps. Their tyres are much taller than you!

Lorry

Rubbish truck

Heavy-duty electric truck

Snow plough

Military truck

Flatbed truck loaded with straw

Billboard truck

Fuel truck

Electric truck

Dekotora trucks are from Japan. They are decorated from top to bottom with paint and neon lights.

Road train

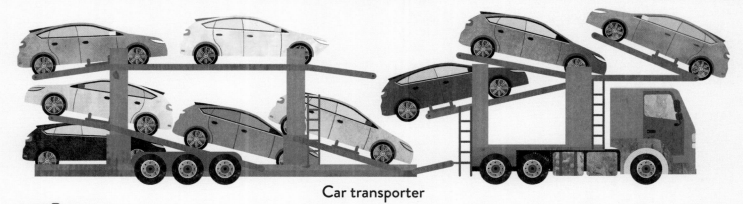
Car transporter

Trucks

Rubbish trucks and mining trucks, transporter trucks and pick-up trucks — trucks can be large or small, and take things where they need to go. Beep, beep!

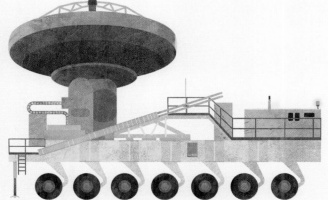
Telescope antenna transporter

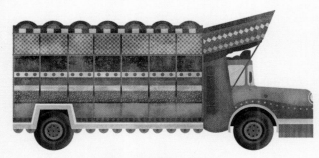
Pakistani jingle trucks are covered in bells and chains that jingle.

Christmas tree truck

Amphibious trucks can drive on land and also go in the water.

Rusty old pick-up truck

Mining truck

Food truck

Recycling truck

Milk float

Shiny new pick-up truck

7

At the Petrol Station

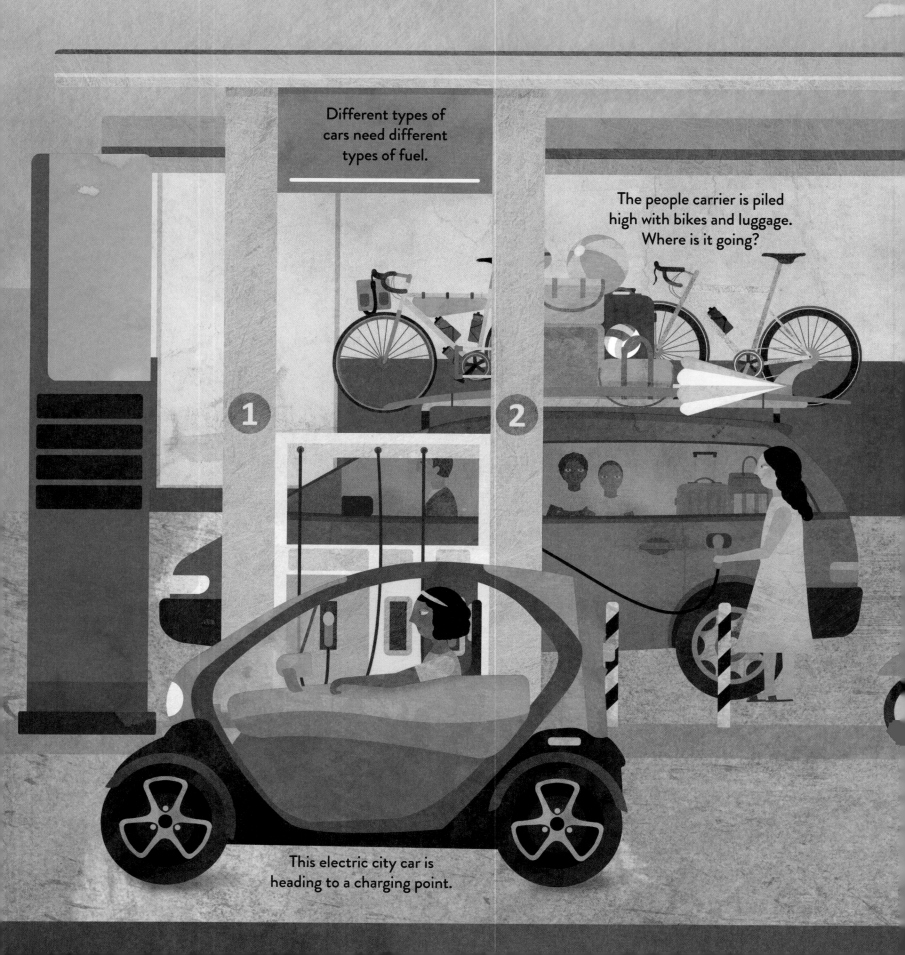

Different types of cars need different types of fuel.

The people carrier is piled high with bikes and luggage. Where is it going?

This electric city car is heading to a charging point.

There are lots of different vehicles here. Everybody needs to **fill up** with fuel before a long journey.

Classic car

London taxi

Dune buggies can drive over sand on the beach.

Rally car

Convertible

Cars, Vans and Buses

Some cars are designed to go as fast as possible, while others are small for busy cities, or big and spacious for large families. Look at the different kinds of buses and taxis that drive passengers.

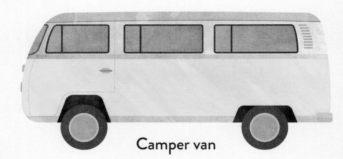
Camper van

People carrier

SUV

Double-decker bus

This **Hotrod** has been painted with flames and given a powerful engine.

Hatchback

Super cars are very fast and extremely expensive.

Stretch limo

City car

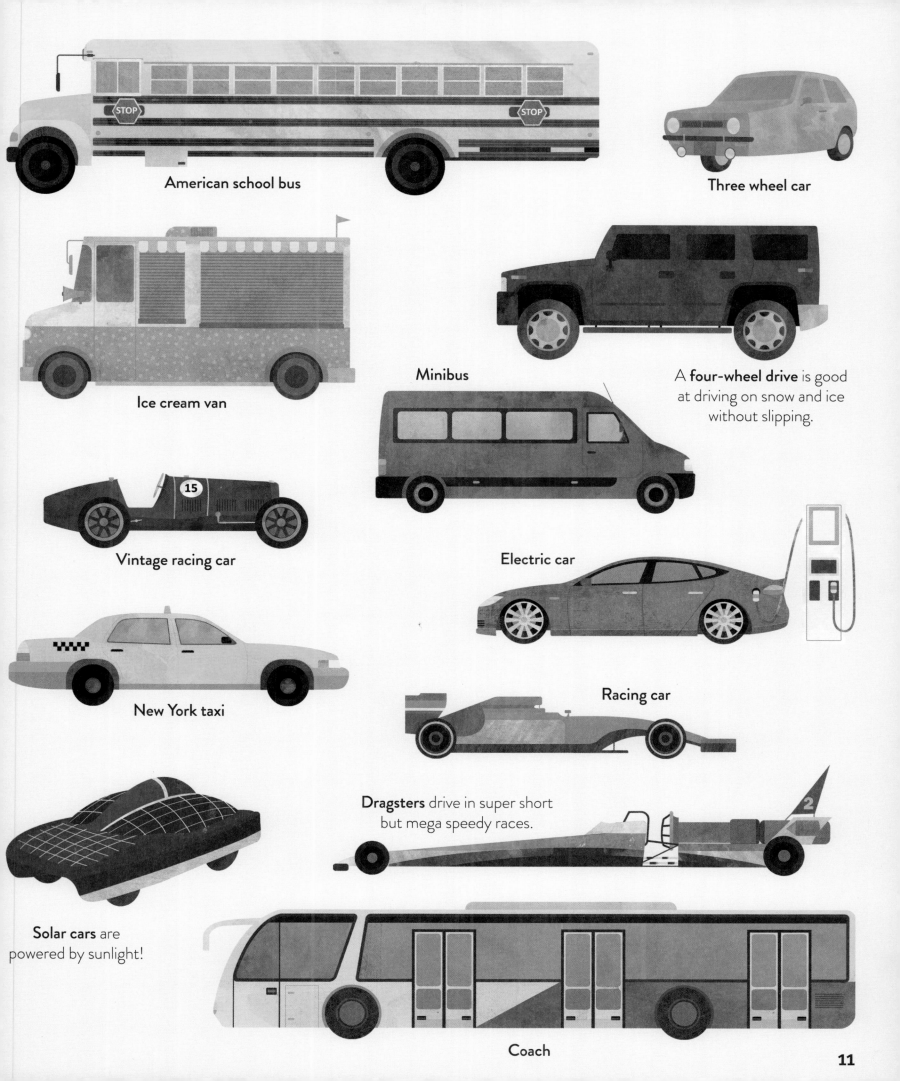

American school bus

Three wheel car

Ice cream van

Minibus

A **four-wheel drive** is good at driving on snow and ice without slipping.

Vintage racing car

Electric car

New York taxi

Racing car

Dragsters drive in super short but mega speedy races.

Solar cars are powered by sunlight!

Coach

Let's Race!

Monster truck

Rally car

Vintage racing car

And they're off!
Which is your
favourite race car?

Sports car

2

9

6

8

16

18

Go-kart

Motorway Mayhem

How many vehicles
with bicycles can
you spot?

Cars and trucks of all different shapes and sizes drive along the motorway. Where are they all going? **Don't get stuck in traffic!**

Construction workers use a roller to flatten new road.

At the Fire Station

A long ladder is extended to reach the fire.

Jets of water shoot out from the hoses to put out the flames!

These firefighters are practising how to put out a fire in a tall building.

More firefighters bring ladders to reach the fire.

This fire engine is about to go to a real emergency! Switch on the flashing lights and sound the siren – it's time to go!

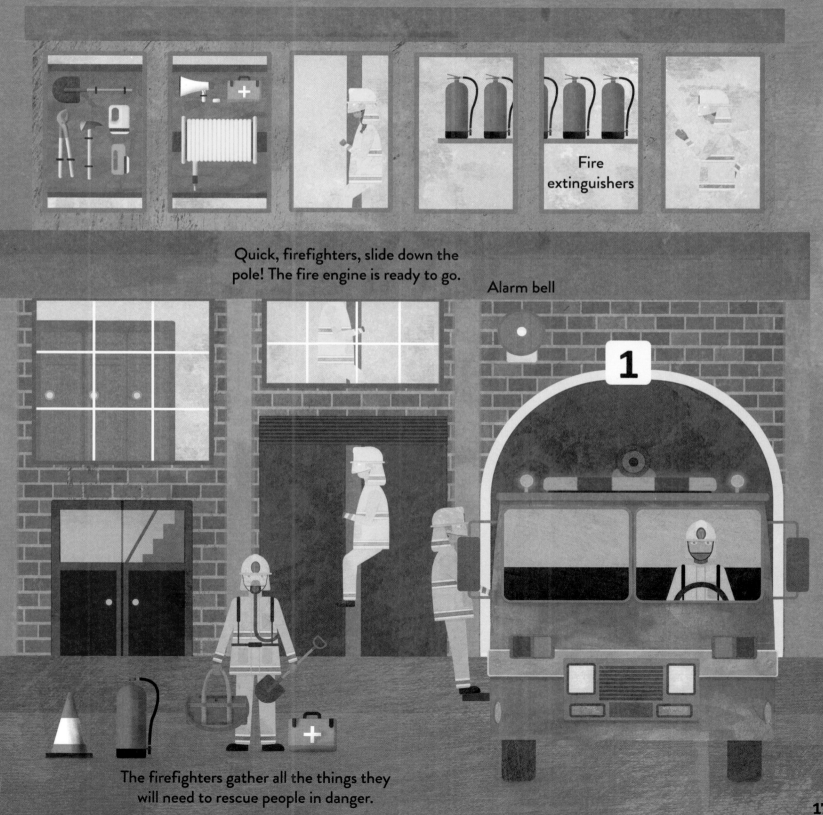

Fire extinguishers

Quick, firefighters, slide down the pole! The fire engine is ready to go.

Alarm bell

1

The firefighters gather all the things they will need to rescue people in danger.

Inside a Fire Engine

Deluge gun

Tools

Fire station dog

Pump panel

Helmet

Hose

Firefighters store all the equipment they need inside a fire engine. Everything has its proper place. **What can you see?**

Ladder

Fire extinguisher

First aid kit

Emergency!

Would you rather be a firefighter in a shiny red truck, a police officer with flashing sirens, or a paramedic, rushing to help those who are sick or injured?

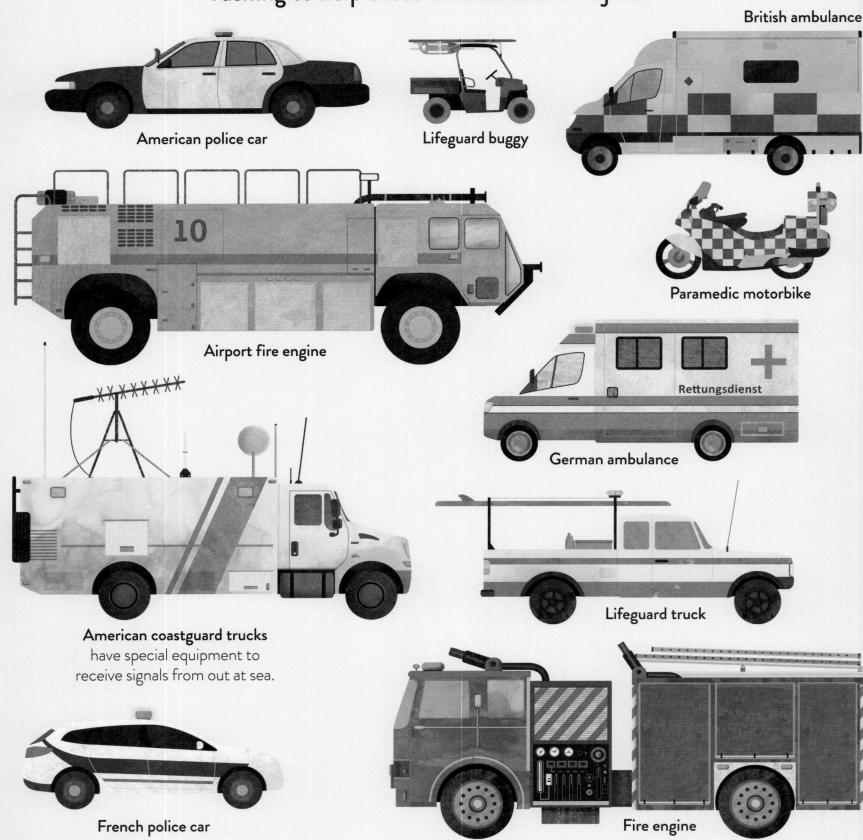

American police car

Lifeguard buggy

British ambulance

Airport fire engine

10

Paramedic motorbike

German ambulance

Rettungsdienst

Lifeguard truck

American coastguard trucks have special equipment to receive signals from out at sea.

French police car

Fire engine

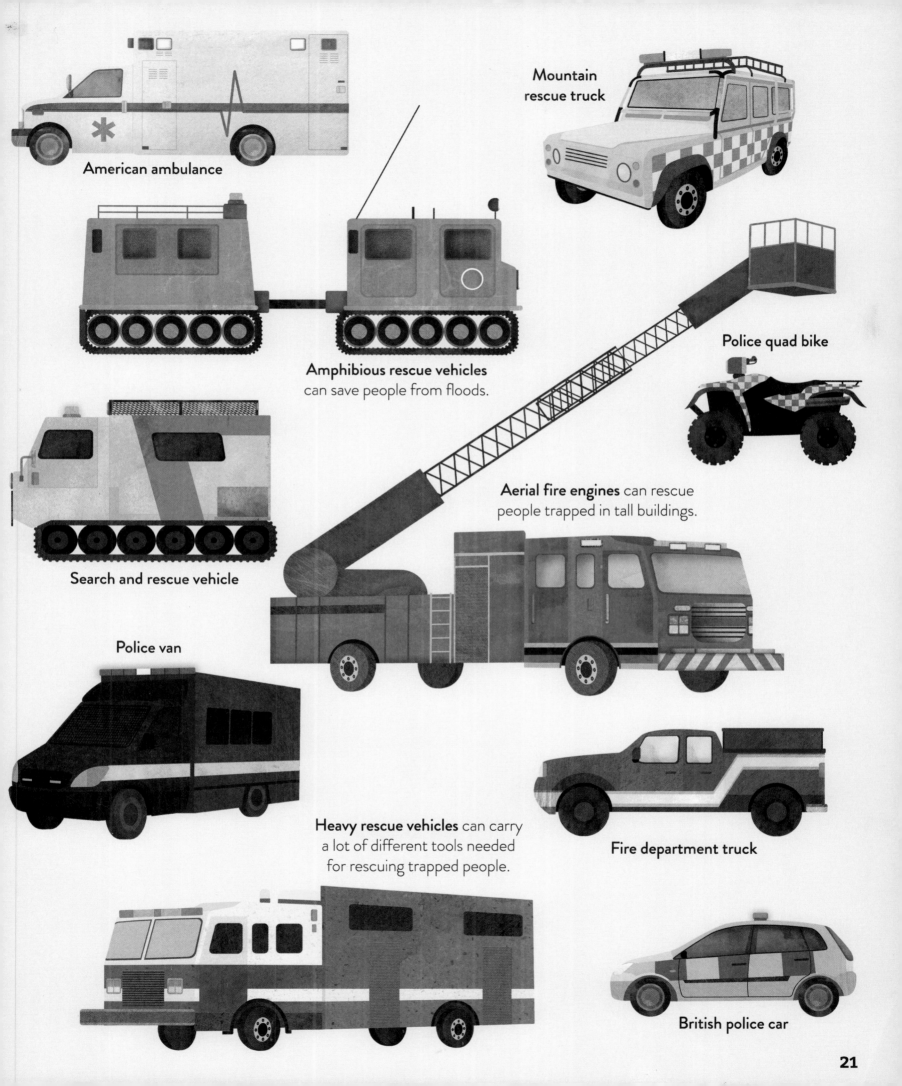

American ambulance

Mountain rescue truck

Amphibious rescue vehicles can save people from floods.

Police quad bike

Aerial fire engines can rescue people trapped in tall buildings.

Search and rescue vehicle

Police van

Heavy rescue vehicles can carry a lot of different tools needed for rescuing trapped people.

Fire department truck

British police car

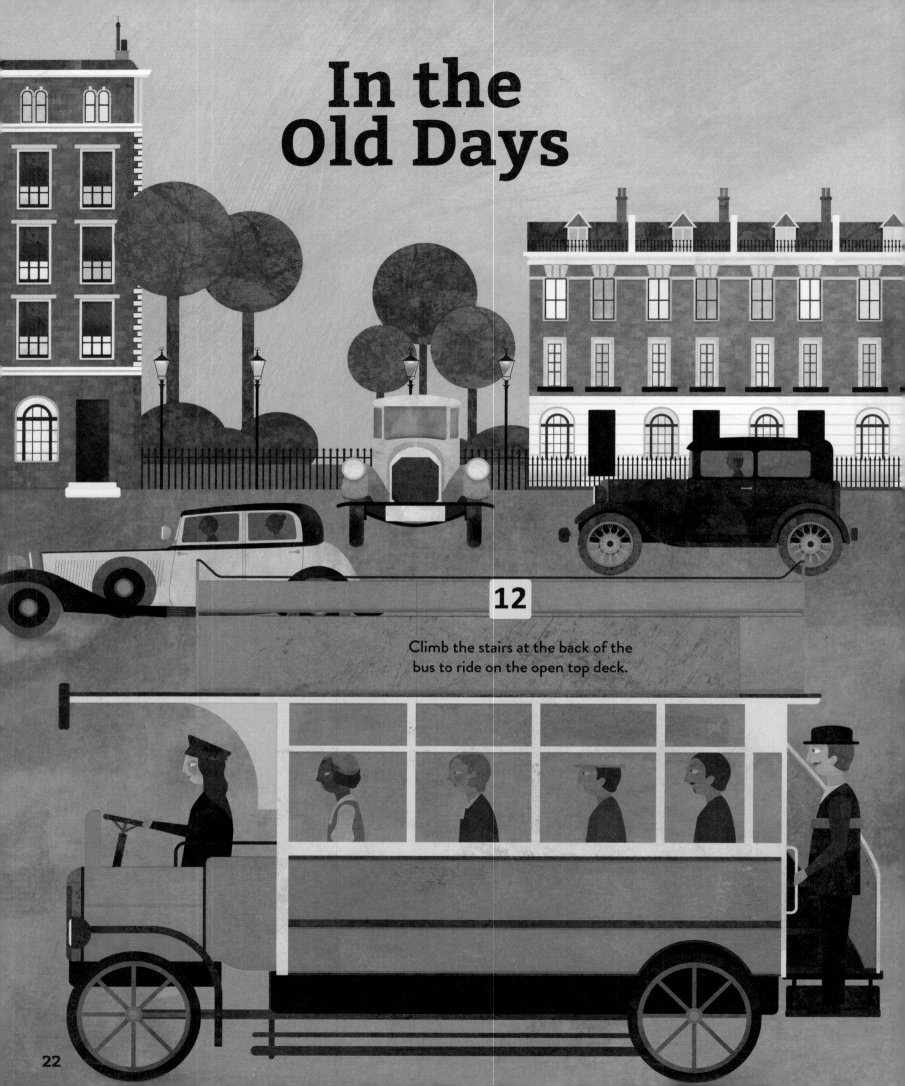

In the Old Days

12

Climb the stairs at the back of the bus to ride on the open top deck.

Toot toot! People have been driving cars for more than a hundred years. They looked a bit different back then.

Instead of traffic lights, a traffic policeman tells cars when to go.

Car horn

Spare tyre

23

Track bicycle

Electric bikes have a motor that helps you cycle up hills.

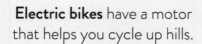

Racing motorbike

You need good balance to ride a **unicycle.**

Stunt bike

Taxi bike

Tricycle

Child's bicycle

You can learn to do cool tricks on a **BMX.**

Bicycle with child's seat

Harley-Davidson engines are louder than a car!

Classic road bicycle

Motorbike and sidecar

Road bicycle

Sightseeing bicycle

24

Electric scooter

Brilliant Bikes

Bikes can travel on roads, up mountains and even on water! Would you like to ride one with one, two or three wheels?

Folding bicycle

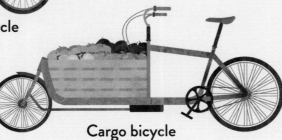
Cargo bicycle

Tuk-tuk

Lie-back tricycle

Mountain bikes have bigger tyres to ride over bumpy ground.

Snowbike

Tandem bicycle

Scooter

Classic bicycle

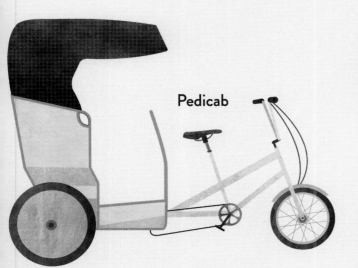
Pedicab

Water bike

Pedal Power

All these people are out for a bike ride. It's hard work going uphill, but lots of fun **whizzing back down!**

Unicycle

Pedicab

Tandem bicycle

Everyone wears a
helmet to keep them
safe if they fall off
their bicycle.

BMX

Would you enjoy
zooming down a
steep hill?

Milk tanker

Cabless tractor

Quad bikes have thick tyres to help them drive over soft or muddy ground.

Mini loader

Tracked tractor

Tractor with snow plough

On the Farm

Tractors and trucks have all sorts of jobs to do on the farm. Some carry animals, others help to plant and harvest crops. Which would you like to drive?

Tractor with bale loader

Tractor with plough

Combine harvesters have a ladder to help the drivers climb into the cab.

Skid steer loader

Digger

Pick-up truck

Tractor

Tractor with mower

Tractor with grapple fork
to move fallen trees.

Animal transporter

Four-wheel drive

Tractor with trailer

Straw baler

Rotary hoe

Tractor with
loader

Tractor with manure spreader

Where do you think the horse
in this **horse truck** is going?

Inside an Ice Cream Van

Can you hear that jingle? It's the ice cream van!

Sprinkles

Loudspeaker

Sauces

Which flavour ice cream would you choose?
Sprinkles or sauce on top?

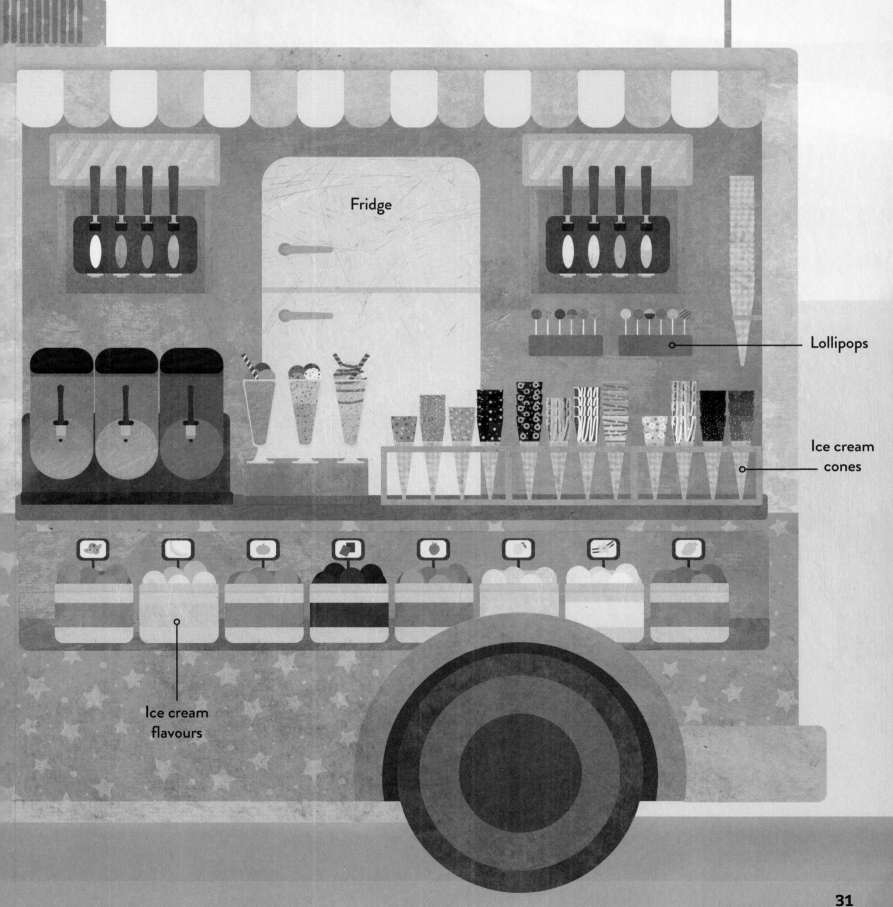

Fridge

Lollipops

Ice cream cones

Ice cream flavours

Eurostar

Steam train

Funicular trains can carry people up very steep hills and mountains.

Passenger train

Diesel shunter

High-speed train

Double-decker train

Indian mountain train

Miniature train

This **snow plough train** has a pointed bit at the front that pushes the snow off the track.

Vintage tram

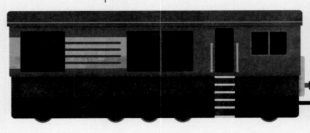

Monorail

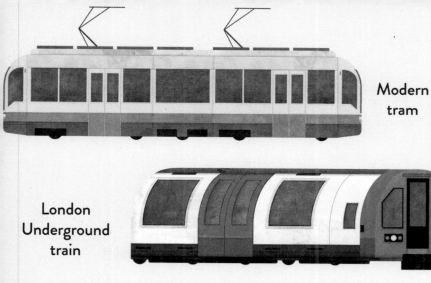
Modern tram

Firefighter train

London
Underground
train

Trains

Trains run on tracks, and can travel long distances without getting stuck in traffic. They can be powered by steam, diesel or electricity.

High-speed steam locomotive

Diesel engine

French Metro train

Japanese bullet trains are super speedy! They are the fastest type of train.

Freight train

American steam
locomotive

Italian
train

American
subway train

33

Construction Vehicles

These machines can build anything, from long, flat roads to the tallest towers. Some have gigantic wheels, some have long arms to dig or push dirt, some have trays to carry heavy loads. Look at all the amazing tools they use!

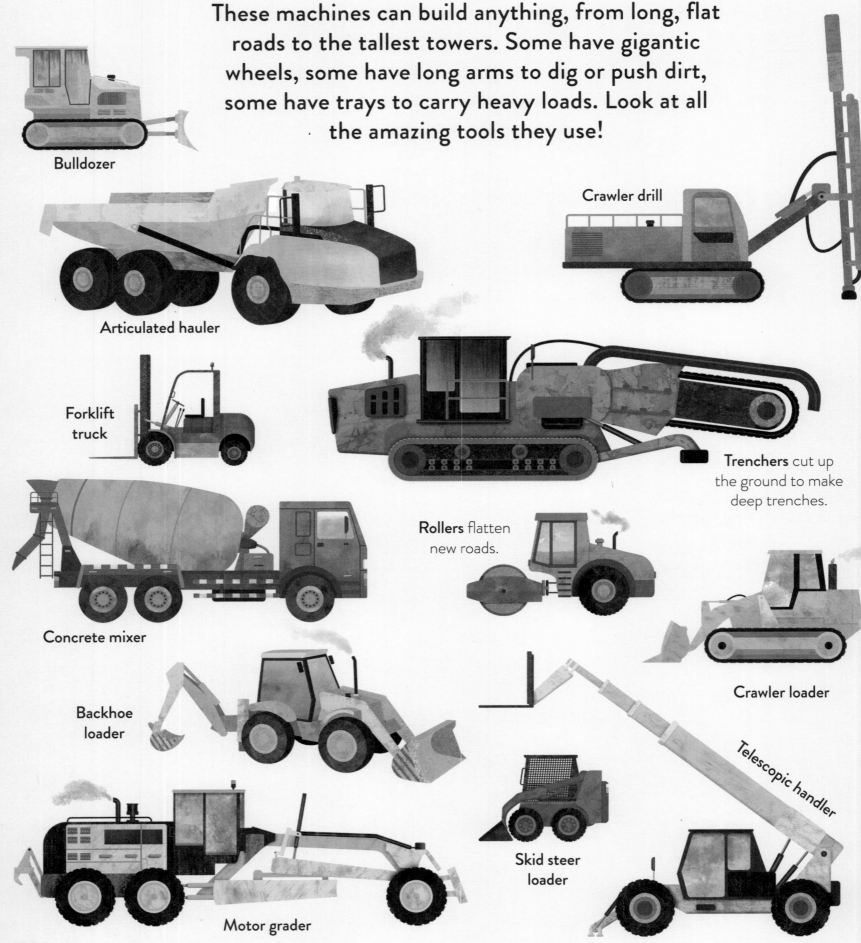

Bulldozer

Articulated hauler

Crawler drill

Forklift truck

Trenchers cut up the ground to make deep trenches.

Concrete mixer

Rollers flatten new roads.

Crawler loader

Backhoe loader

Telescopic handler

Skid steer loader

Motor grader

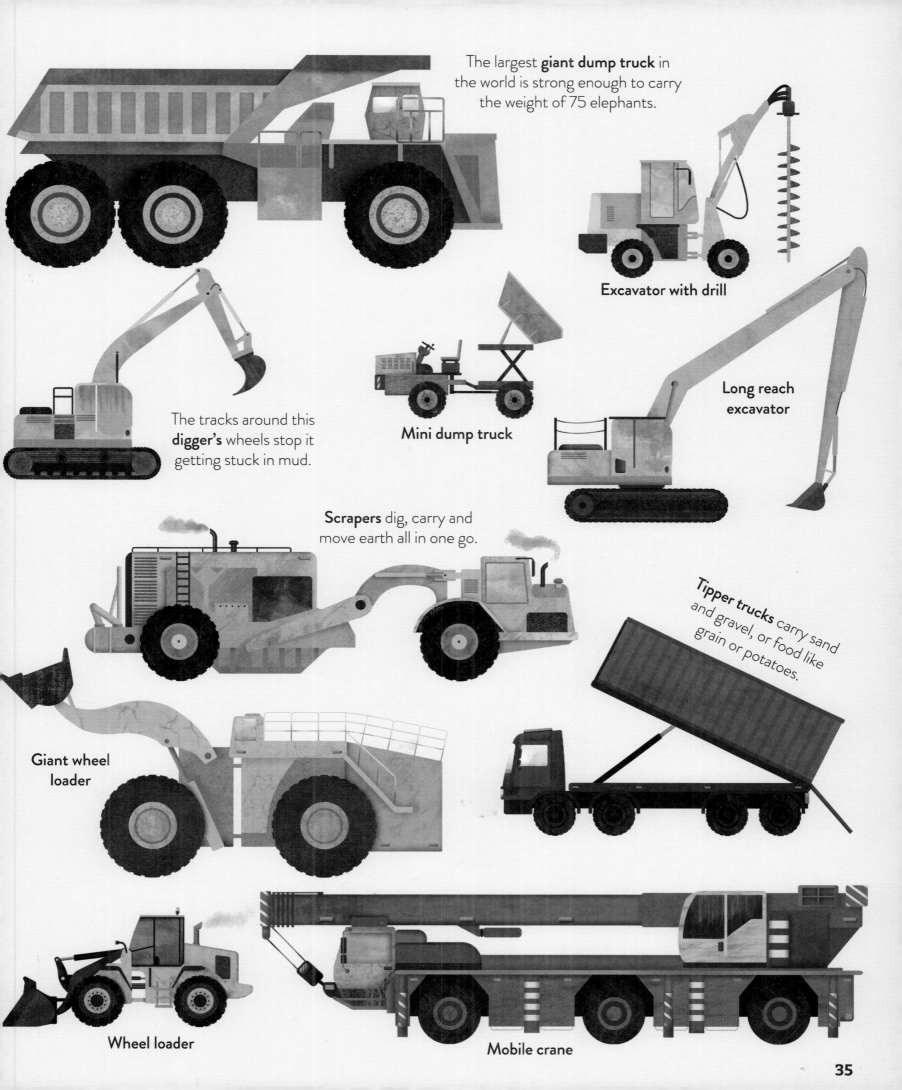

The largest **giant dump truck** in the world is strong enough to carry the weight of 75 elephants.

Excavator with drill

The tracks around this **digger's** wheels stop it getting stuck in mud.

Mini dump truck

Long reach excavator

Scrapers dig, carry and move earth all in one go.

Tipper trucks carry sand and gravel, or food like grain or potatoes.

Giant wheel loader

Wheel loader

Mobile crane

Inside a Freight Train

Freight trains can be hundreds of carriages long!

Grain

8237

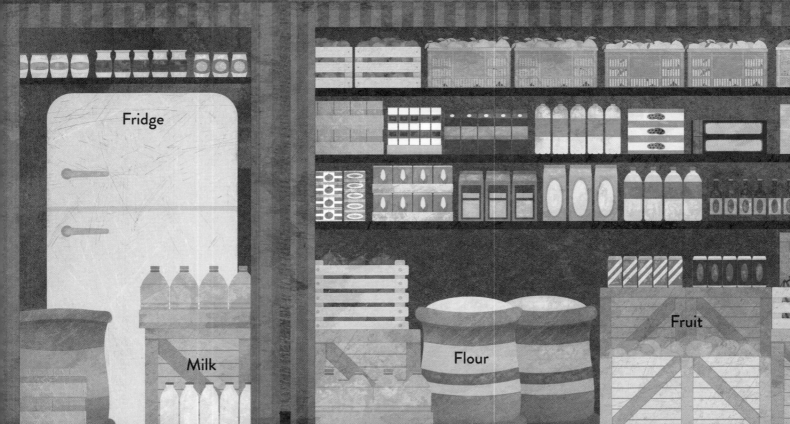

Fridge

Milk

Flour

Fruit

Freight trains are filled with all sorts of things. They travel long distances, carrying different cargo from place to place. What's inside this one?

Coal

Oil tank car

Cars

Tracks

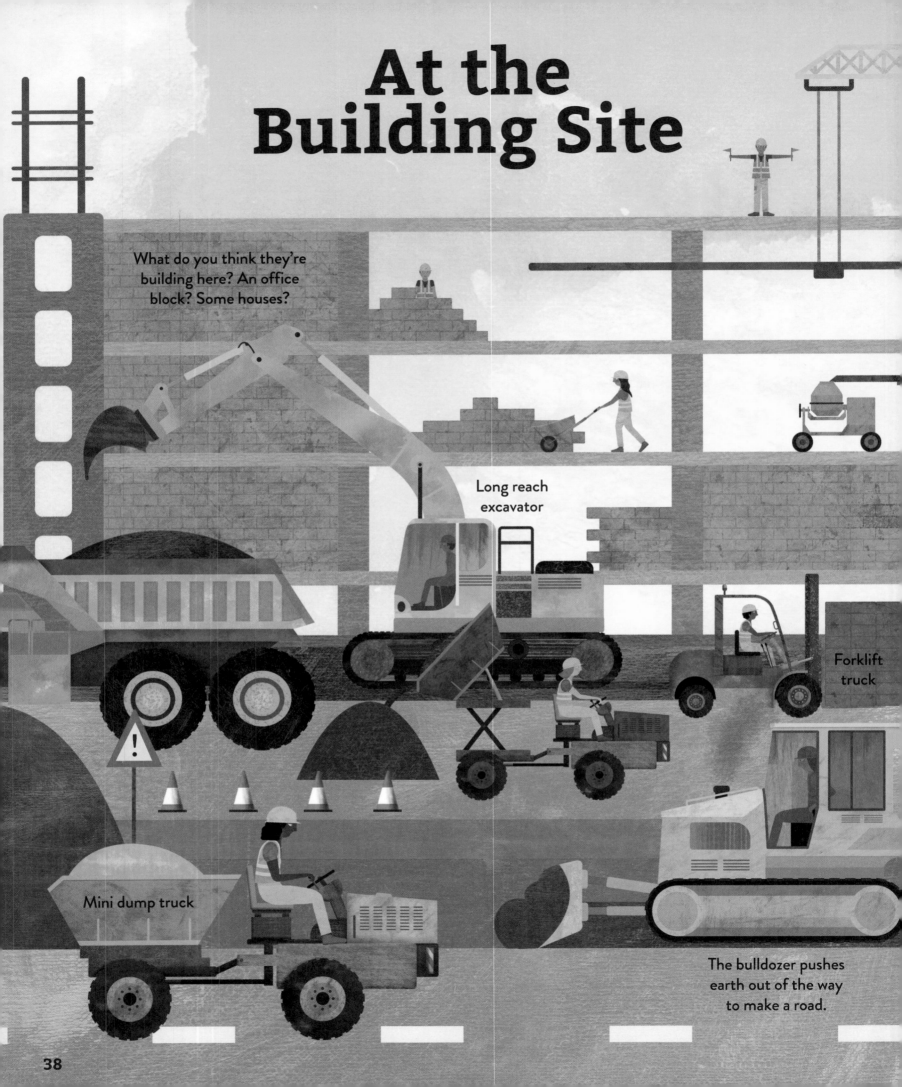

At the Building Site

What do you think they're building here? An office block? Some houses?

Long reach excavator

Forklift truck

Mini dump truck

The bulldozer pushes earth out of the way to make a road.

The machines are hard at work digging, dumping and building things on the construction site. They all have to work together as a team to **get the jobs done.**

Crane

Concrete mixer

This tipper truck is unloading gravel.

Roller

At the Airport

AIRPORT TERMINAL

Passenger transport bus

Windsocks show pilots which way the wind is blowing and how strong it is.

Plane refueler truck

A1

Luggage carrier

It's very busy at the airport. Trucks drive here and there making sure the planes are ready for take off.

People in the air traffic control tower tell the planes when they can take off and land.

Monorail

10

Airport fire engine

Passengers use aircraft stairs to board the plane.

A2

This truck is unloading food for the passengers on the plane.

Catering truck

At the Scrapyard

Vehicles are stacked on metal frames so mechanics can find parts that still work.

A long-armed machine picks up cars ready to crush them.

Old, used vehicles are brought to the scrapyard to be taken apart and recycled. It's full of car parts and tyres.

These cars are crushed flat to make more space in the scrap yard.

Beep, beep! Watch out – this bulldozer is coming through!

Wheely Fun Facts

1. Monster trucks can do huge jumps. The longest ever monster truck jump was over 72 metres long. That's about the length of 15 cars!

2. The longest road train ever was almost 1.5 kilometres long. It would take you about 18 minutes to walk from one end to the other.

3. The highest backflip on a bicycle was 2.8 metres high.

4. A car exists that's in the shape of a hotdog, and it's called the Wienermobile!

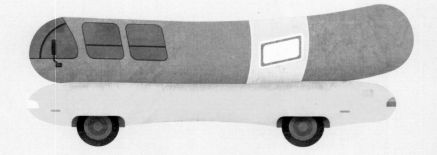

5. The fastest ever car is called Thrust SSC and it travelled at 1,228 kilometres an hour. That's about 10 times faster than a family car would drive on a motorway.

6. The smallest car ever made is called the Peel P50. It only has one door and one headlight, and it can be picked up!

7. Diggers can dance! There is a group of huge diggers that can perform tricks, spins and wave their buckets in the air to music.

8. Bagger 293 is an enormous bucket-wheel excavator. It uses buckets to scoop up earth and then drop it on conveyor belts to carry it away. Weighing in at 14,196 tonnes, it is the largest and heaviest land vehicle on Earth.

9. The longest passenger train is called The Ghan and it runs across Australia. It can have as many as 44 carriages and is over 770 metres long.

10. There's enough train track in India to circle the Earth almost three times.

Can You Spot?

Take a look through the book and see which of these items and vehicles you can find!

Trophy

Helmet

Electric scooter

Unicycle

Concrete mixer

Quad bike

Ladder

Luggage truck

Ice cream sundae

Camper van

Tyres

Christmas tree

Traffic policeman

Go-kart

Charging point

Mini dump truck

Paramedic motorbike

Miniature train

Car wash

Fire station dog

Traffic cone
How many traffic cones can
you spot in the book?

Vrooom vrooom!